In
A GRAND DAY OUT
BY NICK PARK

EGMONT

We bring stories to life

First published in Great Britain 2009
by Egmont UK Limited
239 Kensington High Street, London W8 6SA

© and ™ Aardman Animations Ltd. 2009. All rights reserved
Wallace and Gromit © and ™ Aardman Animations Limited
A Grand Day Out © NFTS 1989
Based on characters created by Nick Park

Illustrated by David Lopez
Edited by Beth Harwood
Designed by Andrea Pollock

ISBN 978 1 4052 4532 6
1 3 5 7 9 10 8 6 4 2

Printed in Singapore

In
A GRAND DAY OUT
BY NICK PARK

ILLUSTRATED BY DAVID LOPEZ

FOREWARD BY NICK PARK

It's fascinating to see this adaptation of 'A Grand Day Out' because I originally planned Wallace & Gromit as a graphic novel. I was trying to find ways to make money when I was at art school and wanted to create adventures like Tintin, but with the warmth of Raymond Briggs' books. I made a start on a couple of stories, but they didn't go that far. They were about Mr Norris and his pet cat, Gromit – Mr Norris had a bicycle that could fly when he turned the front light on! There was another character, a postman called Jerry, who actually looked a bit like Wallace.

Then, when I was searching for a subject for my graduation film at the National Film and Television School, I hit upon the idea of a guy who builds a rocket in his basement. I thought he needed someone to talk to – a pet or something – and I found Gromit the cat in my old sketchbooks. But I changed him to a dog because it was easier to make out of Plasticine – I couldn't put a brow on a cat, but it worked on a dog! And I changed the guy's name from Jerry to Wallace.

I wrote a script with a friend, Steve Rushton. It was about 20 pages long, but it would have taken nine years to make it the way it was. The first sentence I started filming – "Wallace and Gromit now build a rocket" – took me a year and a half to do, so I reworked the storyboard. We were going to have a big scene in a McDonald's on the Moon with aliens in it like the cantina in 'Star Wars', but I simplified this to have them upset a robot who looks after the Moon.

I eventually ran out of time at the NFTS, but Peter Lord and David Sproxton invited me to come and work for them at Aardman, where they were making Morph, and pop videos like Peter Gabriel's 'Sledgehammer'. They let me have a corner of the studio to finish 'A Grand Day Out', which took another four years because I was only working part-time on it.

I had the feeling it was something special, but in the gap before post-production I made 'Creature Comforts' for Aardman's 'Lip Synch' series. Both films got nominated for an Oscar® – I didn't even know there was an Oscar® for Short Animation! – and 'Creature Comforts' won, so it stole the limelight from Wallace & Gromit. It was only when the BBC commissioned 'The Wrong Trousers' and bought 'A Grand Day Out' as part of the package that it really took off.

Looking back 20 years later, I still pinch myself – this daft idea I had at art school is now a household name. I don't know if I'll ever quite get used to it. But it's great to see this graphic novel as a reminder of how it all began.

Nick Park

January 2009

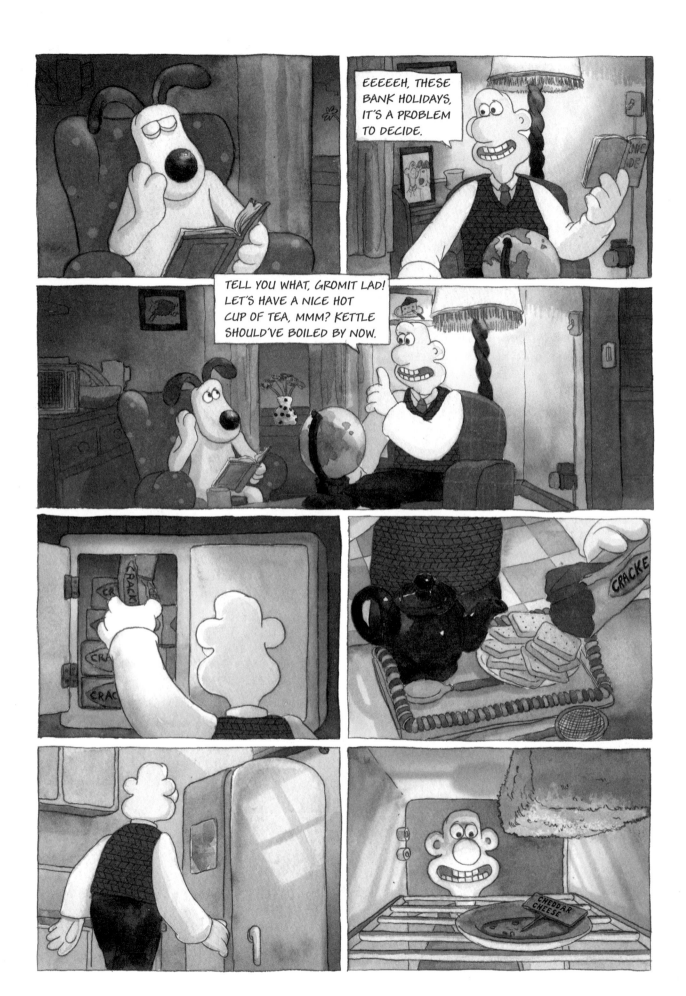

. . . EVERYBODY KNOWS THE MOON'S MADE OF CHEESE!

EEK, EEK!

DUM-DE-DUM, DUM . . .

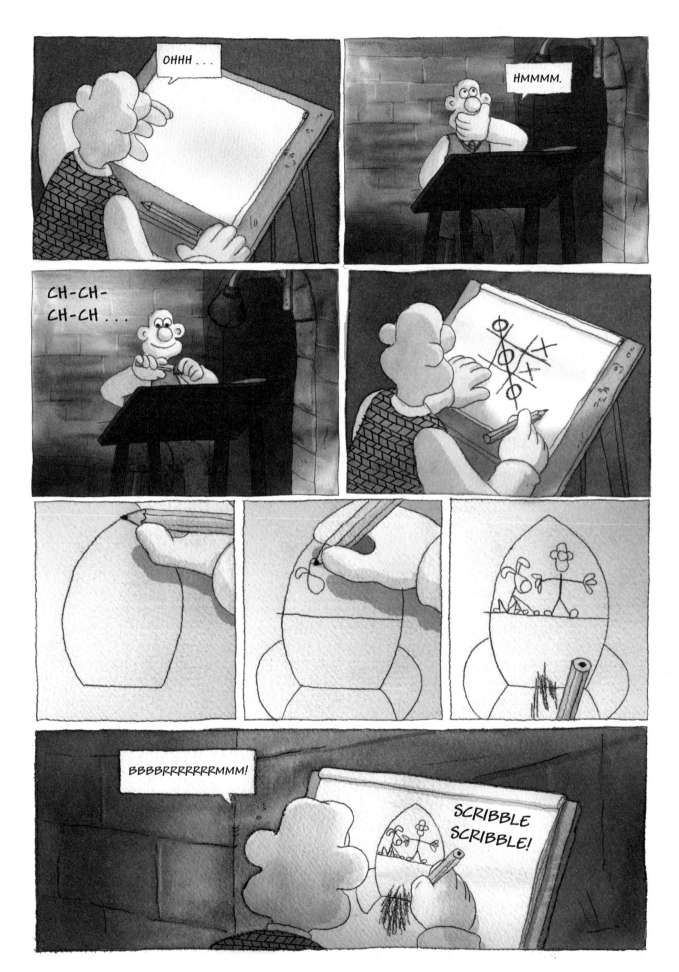

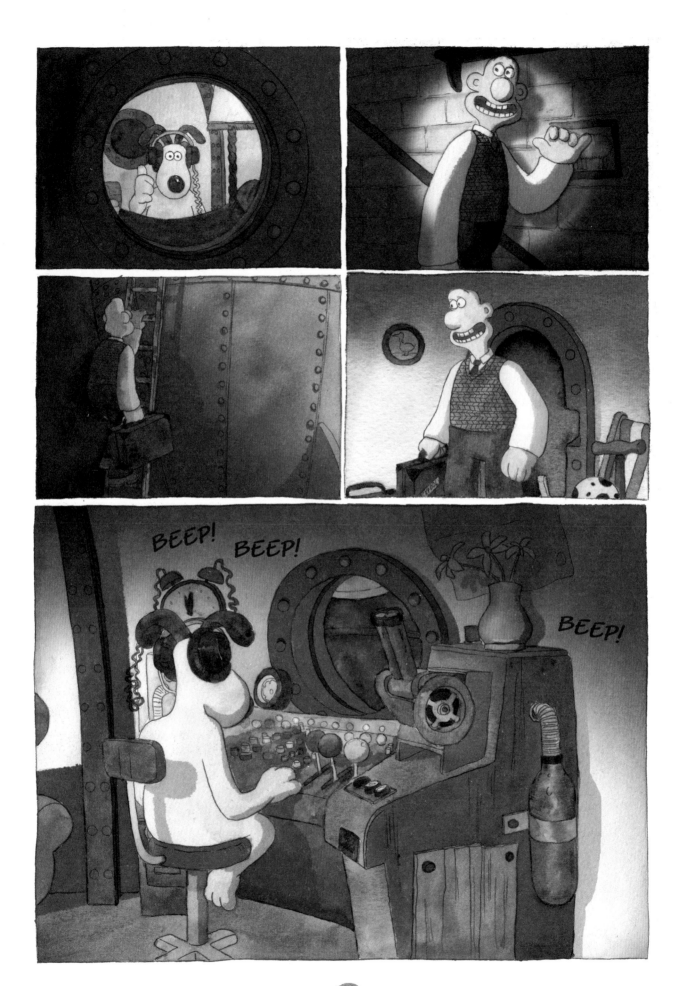

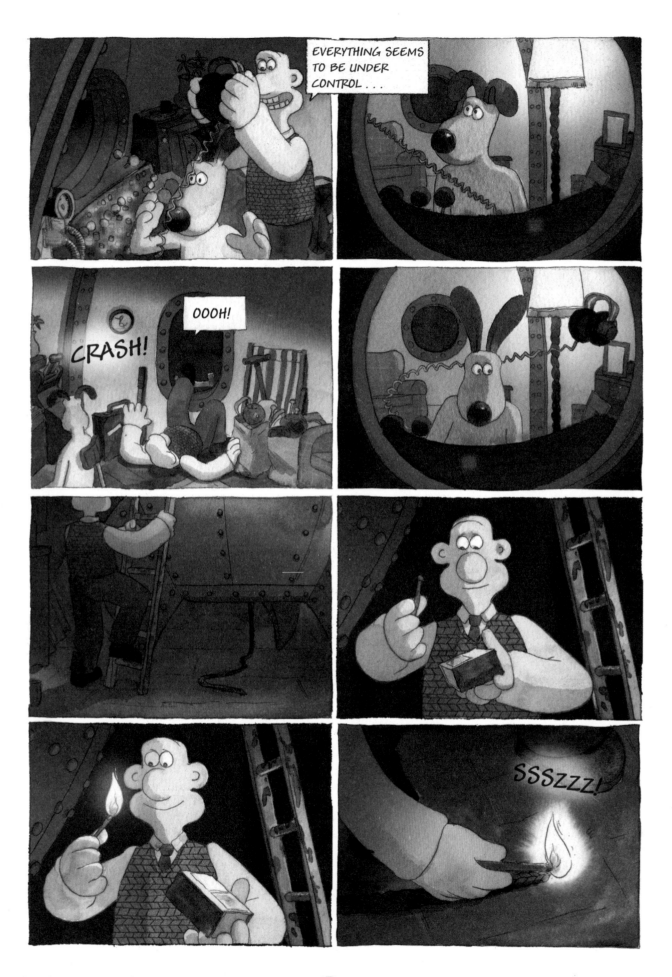

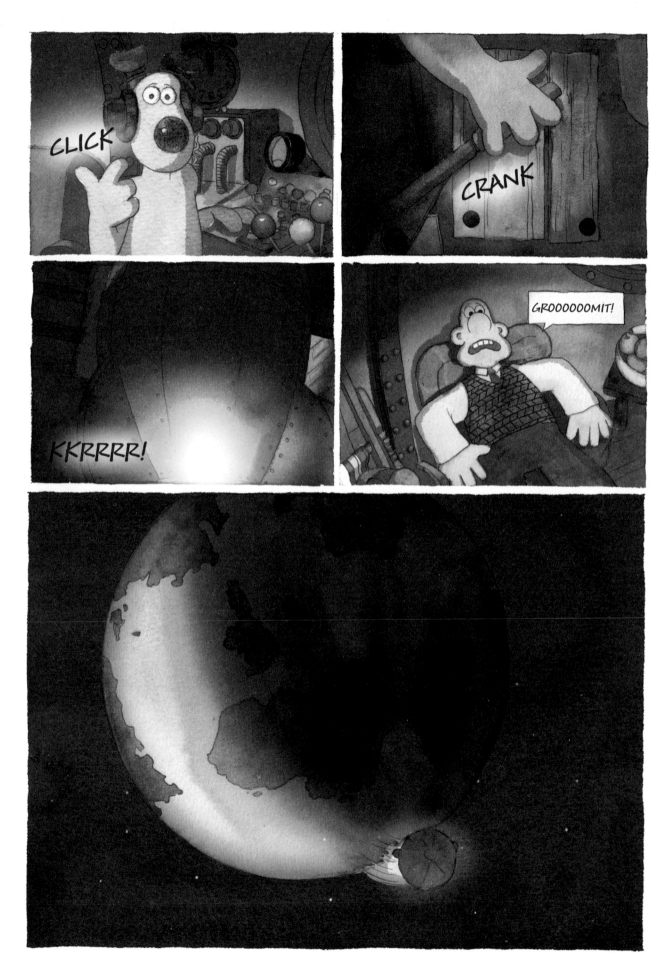

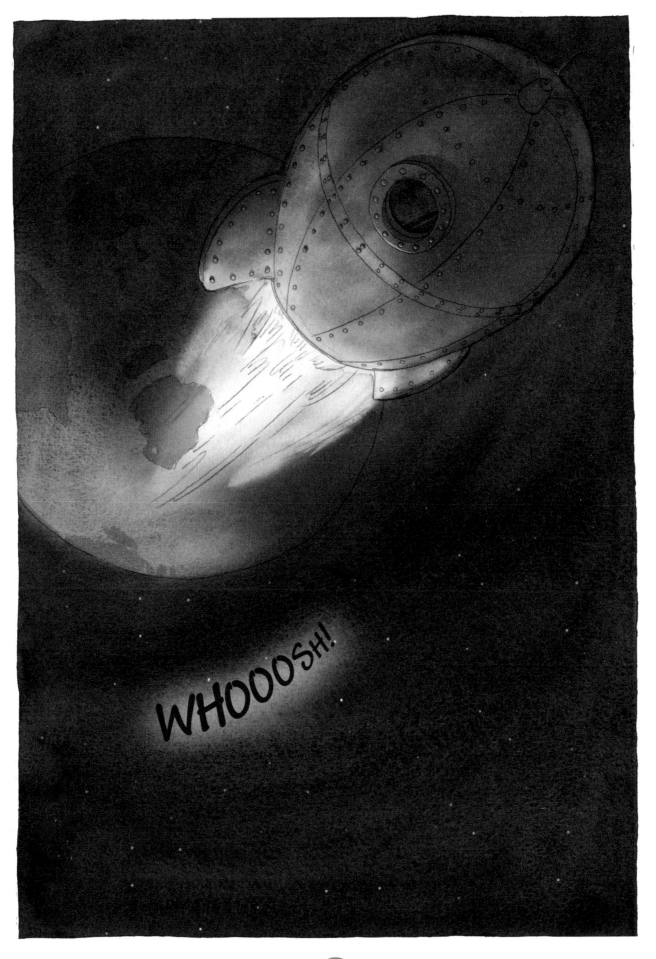

ONE FOR THE ALBUM!

CLICK!

BEEP! BLIP! BEEP! BLIP!

21

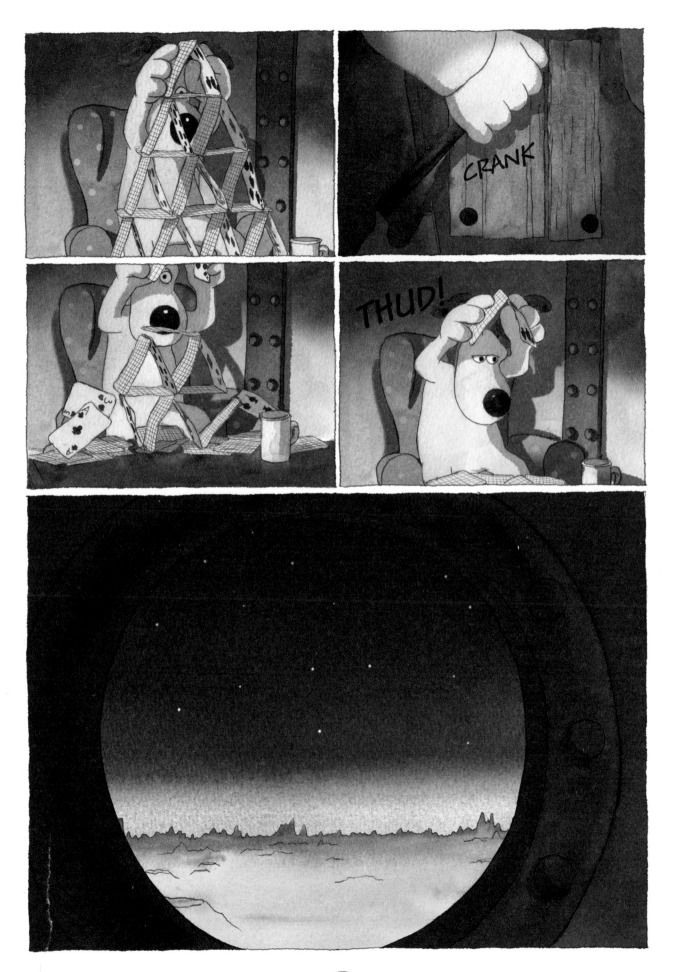

CRANK

THUD!

BOOIINN . . .

OH!?

NICE DROP OF TEA TO GET THE TASTE BUDS GOING.

MMMM!

PLATE?

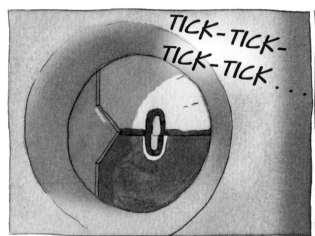

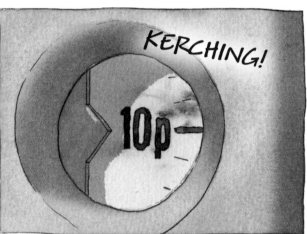

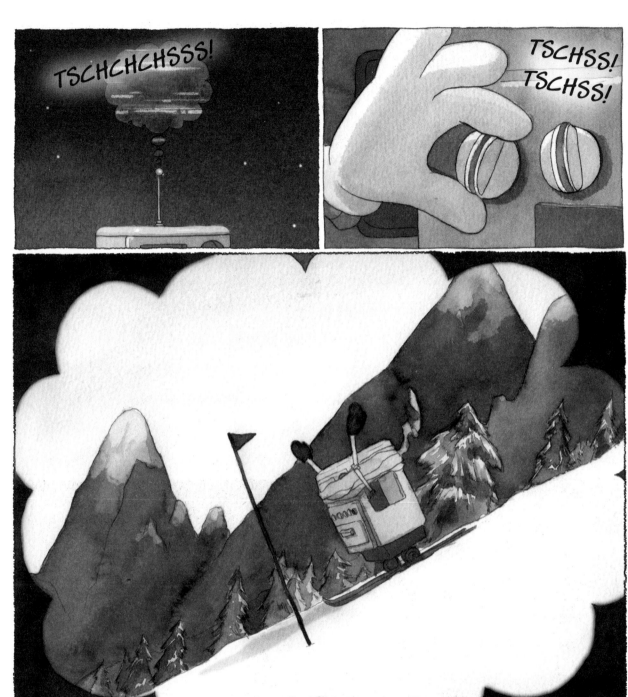

SPLOOP!

SPLAT!

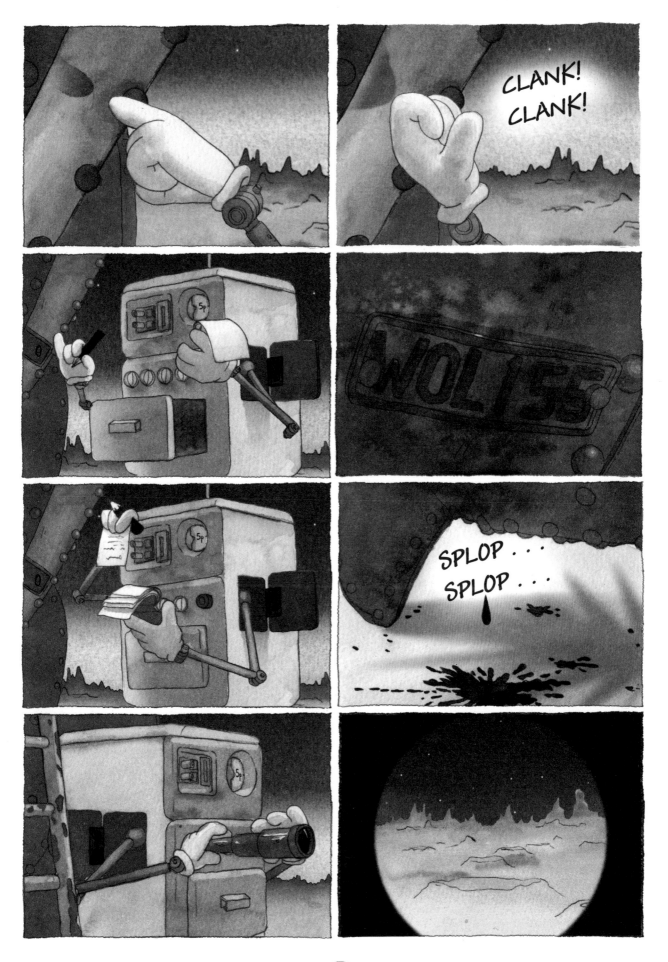

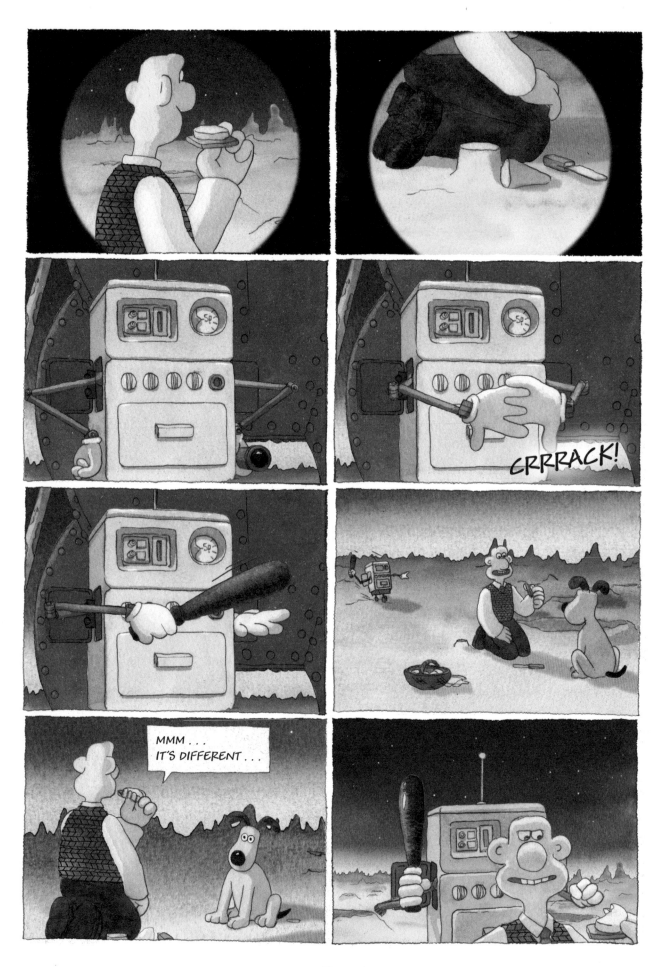

CRRRACK!

MMM . . .
IT'S DIFFERENT . . .

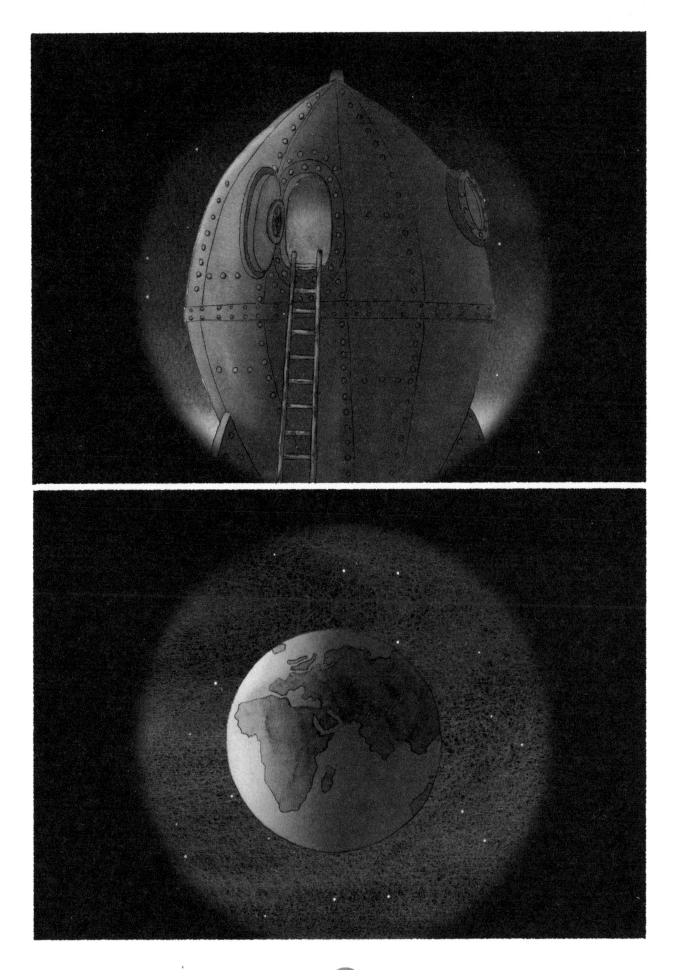

EEK-EEK!
EEK-EEK!

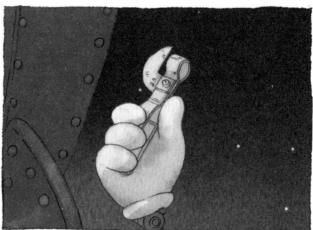

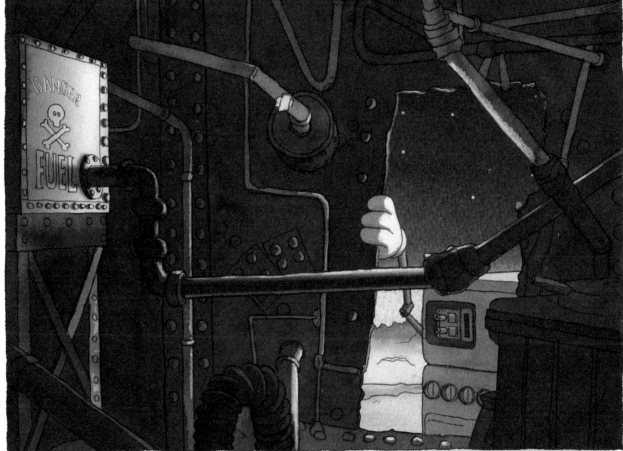

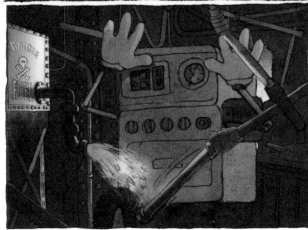

43

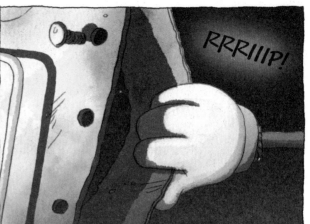

RRRIIIP!

CRRREEEAK!

BRRRING!

OOOHHHHH!

46

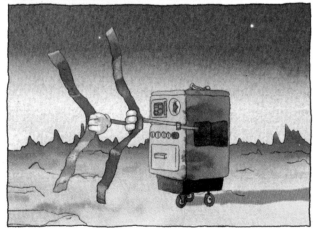

CLUNK!

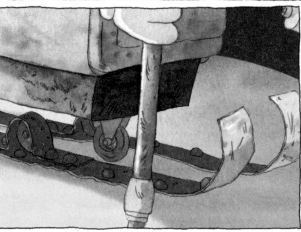

50

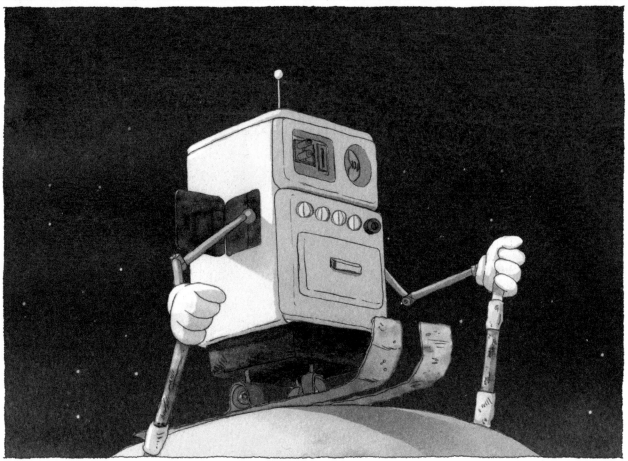

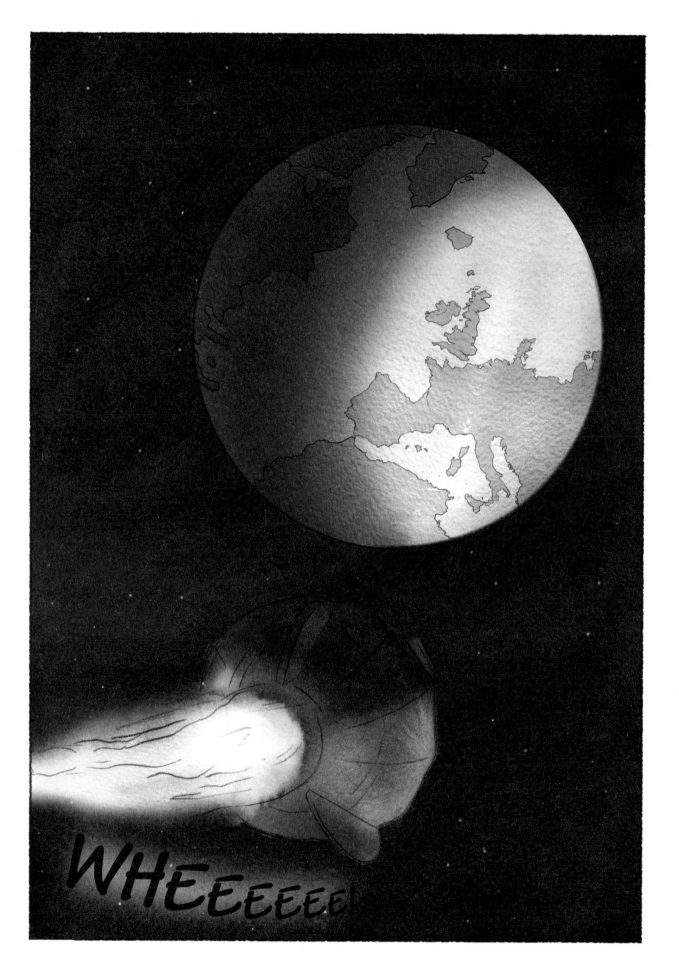

THE
END

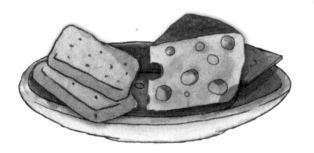